Mocha Moments

Constantia Corner Café Book 2

Nina Potter

Get Your Free Book!

Sign up for my newsletter and as a thank-you, I'll send you a free novella.

It's a story close to my heart, filled with the kind of genuine, later-in-life romance that I love writing about.

Plus, you'll get a regular dose of updates, insights, and maybe a few surprises along the way.

No spam, just stories.

Interested?

Sign up and let's dive into this journey together.

Contents

1. Prologue: Jack — 1
2. Lisa — 6
3. David — 13
4. Lisa — 23
5. David — 31
6. Lisa — 40
7. David — 49
8. Lisa — 58
9. David — 67
10. Epilogue: Jack — 76
Leave a Review — 84

Get Your Free Book!	85
Read More By Nina	86
About Nina Potter	88
Copyright	91

Prologue: Jack

The aroma of freshly baked croissants and brewed coffee enveloped Jack as he stepped behind the counter of the Constantia Corner Café. He breathed in deeply, taking a moment to savor the scents that had become so familiar over the years. This cozy café had been his labor of love ever since leaving the military two decades ago. Now, as the evening crowd filtered in, Jack felt that familiar sense of pride in the community hub he had built.

He glanced around at the patrons absorbed in their own worlds. In the back corner was Lisa, her chestnut hair falling softly around her face. There was a distant look in her eyes, more than just the weariness of a long day. As she flipped through a fashion magazine, Jack couldn't help but wonder if the pages reminded her of a life she once dreamed of, now altered by her recent divorce. She was a regular at the café, often stopping by after work or on weekends. A few tables over, Dr. David Pace was deeply immersed in his notes. The furrow in his brow and the occasional deep sigh told Jack there was more on his mind than just work, the loss of his wife still a shadow in his heart. He came here less often, usually for a quick coffee before heading home.

Jack, while arranging a tray of cinnamon rolls, observed Lisa and David. In the soft glow of the café, he saw not just patrons, but two souls on parallel paths of healing. He saw Lisa's poise and grace, reminiscent of her fashion-forward boutique, and David's contemplative gaze, hinting at a depth formed by past loss. Watching them, Jack felt an inkling of possibility—two souls, each silently nursing their own wounds, yet perhaps unknowingly ready for a new chapter. He wondered if they might find companionship in each other, his matchmaking instincts already stirring.

The café's ambiance shifted subtly as the jazz music, a blend of soulful saxophone and gentle piano, filled the air. The soft evening light cast a warm glow across the walls, adorned with vintage photos and vibrant bookshelves, creating a cozy, inviting space. It was one of Jack's favorite times when the café transformed into a hub of comfort and connection.

His gaze drifted over to Dianne, the talented pastry chef, as she emerged from the kitchen carrying a tray of scones. Jack felt a familiar affection blossom in his chest for Dianne, tinged with a wistful longing, but he held back, wary of crossing the delicate line between personal desires and professional decorum.

Shaking himself back to the present, Jack walked over to greet a few regulars at the counter. "Evening, folks," Jack greeted with a broad smile. "Who's up for Jazz Night this Friday? I hear we've got a saxophonist who can really stir the soul!" The patrons nodded eagerly, already looking forward to the café's popular weekly event. As Jack made his way to Lisa's table with her order, he knew exactly how to spark her interest.

"Evening, Lisa," he said, serving her salted caramel mocha. "You're coming to Jazz Night on Friday, right? The saxophonist this week is supposed to be one of the best we have in Cape Town."

Lisa looked up from her magazine, her hazel eyes reflecting the late evening light. "I was thinking about it," she said. "Could be fun to get out and enjoy some good music."

"You won't regret it," Jack assured with a knowing wink, his tone reflecting the café's warm embrace.

He repeated the process as he went over to David's table for a greeting. "Evening, Dr. Pace," Jack said, noticing the weariness in David's eyes. "You know, the jazz this Friday is the mellow, reflective kind. Might be just the thing for someone who spends his days mending others."

David nodded, his brown eyes crinkling at the corners as he smiled. "I was considering attending," he said in his rich, confident voice. "It's been too long since I've enjoyed some live jazz."

As Jack served other patrons, he mused, *Every story that blooms in this café is unique, yet they all start with that same glimmer of hope, right here amid the coffee and jazz.* Walking back to the counter, his mind began weaving a subtle plan, each step a delicate thread in the tapestry of matchmaking he was so fond of. If he could orchestrate Lisa and David sharing a table during Jazz Night, perhaps they would strike up a connection in the music and ambiance. The café, a haven for many, had always been a crucible for budding romances and enduring friendships, reflecting the current trend of community-centric love stories.

Jack's musings were interrupted as a group got up to leave, smiling gratefully for the warmth of this home away from home. These were the moments that affirmed Jack's purpose here. He treasured being even a small part of so many people's stories.

The remaining evening passed in a pleasant rhythm—greeting customers, serving coffees and pastries, and exchanging the little pleasantries that fed the soul. Before he knew it, the last patron had left and it was time to close up. As Jack wiped down the tables, his thoughts returned to Lisa and David. If Friday night went well, this café could be the first chapter in a story neither of them expected. The prospect filled him with anticipation.

With the chairs neatly stacked and everything in order for tomorrow, Jack headed out. He switched off the lights, casting one last look around and muttering, 'Good night, you old matchmaker,' to the empty café, a hint of humor in his farewell to the day.

Then he stepped out into the night, the faint scent of coffee and croissants lingering on his shirt.

Lisa

The bell above the door chimed softly as Lisa unlocked it and stepped into her boutique. Early morning light filtered through the large front windows, washing over the displays of locally made clothing and accessories. She paused to take in the vibrant colors and textures that greeted her, feeling a swell of pride. This little shop in the heart of Newlands was her sanctuary.

After hanging her coat on the antique rack by the door, Lisa got to work arranging some new pieces that had just arrived. She opened each box slowly, like unwrapping a gift, admiring the artistry of the designers she handpicked. Her fingers traced over the intricate beading on a sundress the color of ripe papaya. She pinned up a hand-dyed silk scarf, its deep jewel tones shimmering in the light.

With each scarf she arranged, Lisa felt a twinge—a reminder of the years she'd spent stifling her creativity in her marriage, and the liberation she'd found in reclaiming it.

Stepping back, she let out a soft sigh, enjoying a quiet moment of satisfaction. In the three years since her divorce, Lisa had poured her heart into this boutique. It was a space entirely her own, where her passion for fashion and eye for beauty could shine. Lisa mused over the newest fashion trend—sustainable, eco-friendly designs. She had always believed in fashion with a conscience, a belief mirrored in the curated collection of her boutique. The pieces she carried were unique, often made locally using traditional methods passed down through generations. She saw herself in the artists she collaborated with—their perseverance, their vision, and their pursuit of meaning in their work.

As Lisa adjusted a display of embroidered shawls, a memory flashed through her mind. The evening she unveiled her boutique idea to her ex-husband, only to be met with disinterest. That moment epitomized the emotional chasm between them, the emotional distance growing wider with each passing year. She and her ex-husband had wanted such different things. He was committed to climbing the corporate ladder, while her dreams were wrapped up in design and creativity. For too long, she had minimized her own desires. The divorce, as painful as it was, opened her eyes to the importance of staying true to oneself. It gave her the courage to leave a job unfulfilling to her soul and open this boutique instead. Here, among these walls, she had found her voice again.

The bell on the door chimed softly as Doris, one of her regular customers, came in. "Good morning, dear!" the elderly woman said warmly. Doris, her silver hair neatly coiffed, had a penchant for stories. "You wouldn't believe the fuss at the bridge club yesterday," she began, her eyes twinkling with the promise of good gossip.

"Doris, so lovely to see you." Lisa smiled. They chatted about the latest gossip, new shawls, and the upcoming artisan trunk show. Lisa's thoughtful recommendations perfectly suited Doris' refined but understated style.

Doris chuckled, adjusting her glasses. "My dear, you always know what suits me. It's like you read my mind." Lisa's laughter mingled with hers. "It's a gift, Doris, one I'm happy to share with you." Watching Doris admire the new silk scarves, Lisa felt a wave of affection for this business she had built through her labor of love.

After Doris left with a cheerful wave, Lisa wandered between the racks, straightening already neat displays. Lisa paused, a silk scarf in her hands, as a couple's laughter echoed from outside. She glanced through the window, a thoughtful expression crossing her face. She hung the scarf with a newfound carefulness as if aligning her thoughts. Her few attempts at dating fizzled out quickly, leaving her wary. She feared letting the wrong person in would disrupt her hard-won independence. But sometimes Lisa wondered if there might still be a companion out there who could truly know her. Someone interested in more than surface-level small talk, who cared to discover the bits of her soul she kept tucked away. She longed for a connection that would nourish the part of herself that her marriage had starved. But the thought of opening up again after past hurt made her pulse quicken with anxiety. With a sigh, she turned away from her musings. There were scarves to be arranged and clothes to price.

In the early afternoon, Mrs. Jacobs, another one of Lisa's regular customers, stepped into the boutique with a hint of worry in her eyes. "Lisa, I need your help," she said. "It's our fortieth anniversary, and I want to surprise my husband with a new look, something different from my usual style. Can you help me?"

Lisa's face brightened. "Of course, Mrs. Jacobs. Let's find something that celebrates your special day and makes you feel fabulous." She guided her customer by selecting pieces that pushed the boundaries of Mrs. Jacobs' usual conservative style, yet remained elegant and comfortable. Mrs. Jacobs had confided in Lisa over the years about her adventures as a young woman traveling the world. "You've helped me rediscover the daring spirit I thought I'd lost," she said with a grateful smile as she tried on a bold new outfit.

While assisting Mrs. Jacobs, a young couple entered, browsing hand in hand. Watching them, a warmth spread through Lisa. "They remind me of young love, full of hope," Mrs. Jacobs remarked, and Lisa nodded, feeling a sense of possibility stir within her.

After ensuring Mrs. Jacobs left the boutique with a joyful spring in her step, Lisa found herself alone with a moment to reflect. She wandered over to the antique oval mirror, a silent witness to the transformations that happened in her store—not just in fashion, but sometimes in life too. The glass cast her reflection back softly, obscuring the fine lines time had etched at the corners of her hazel eyes. She looked elegant today in a cream blouse and forest-green pencil skirt. Her chestnut hair was styled in gentle waves. But she knew external polish could only conceal so much. Within, she was still cautious, fearful. Warmth bloomed in her chest as she thought of this boutique that had become her shield and her form of self-expression. It gave her an anchor in days when she felt adrift. She rearranged a section of the boutique she hadn't touched in months. "Time for a change," she murmured, feeling an unexpected surge of excitement at the thought of altering more than just the displays.

Glancing at her watch, Lisa saw it was nearly closing time. She walked the boutique one last time, allowing herself to admire the unique pieces that filled her with inspiration. As she turned the sign to Closed, she felt a familiar sense of accomplishment. Hard as some days had been, she had built this little dream world for herself and it gave her joy.

Locking up, Lisa took a moment to gaze at the streets of Newlands, feeling more connected than ever. *Perhaps it's time to be a part of this vibrant tapestry, not just a spectator*, she thought, her eyes lingering on the art festival flyers. She paused, thinking what a lovely way it would be to spend a weekend afternoon browsing booths and taking in the local creative talent. For a moment, she considered going but hesitated. Lately, she had declined invitations, preferring the safety of routines. But didn't she owe it to herself to get out and experience this city she loved?

As she got into her car to head home, her thoughts turned to Constantia Corner Café's jazz night on Friday. She had always meant to attend one of these evenings but something held her back. The owner, Jack, seemed sure she would enjoy the music when he mentioned it yesterday, though. Perhaps this Friday it would feel right to go.

Lisa smiled slightly to herself as she drove, picturing the cozy café filled with the melody of live jazz. It had been too long since she had indulged in one of Cape Town's many cultural treasures. The routine drive home seemed to hum with new energy as she anticipated this potential change to her usual schedule.

A part of her was still afraid—of disappointment, of getting hurt. But a growing part of her felt ready to take a chance again.

David

David Pace stood motionless in the dimming light of his clinic, the day's last patient having just left. The silence was a stark contrast to the earlier flurry of activity, a daily reminder of the void that had grown in his life. As he locked the door, his gaze lingered on the empty waiting room, each chair a silent witness to the loneliness that shadowed him since his wife's passing. It was in these quiet moments, between the demands of his medical practice and the solitude of his home, that the weight of her absence felt most profound.

The late afternoon sun slanted through the windows, casting the interior in a warm glow as the city began its transition into evening. He slowly made his way through the building, meticulously turning off lights and ensuring everything was in order for tomorrow. As a general practitioner, order and routine brought him comfort, qualities mirrored in the tidy and efficient nature of his practice. Reaching his personal office, he stepped inside, the smell of leather-bound medical books and sanitizer familiar and somehow reassuring.

Sitting down at his desk, David glanced at the framed photo of his late wife. Her smile, forever captured in a moment of laughter, seemed to mock his solemn mood. "You'd tell me to lighten up, wouldn't you?" he murmured to the photo, a small, rueful smile tugging at his lips despite himself. David's gaze drifted from the photo to the empty space beside his desk. For a moment, he was transported back to a late evening years ago, the memory unfolding like a scene from a movie.

'You're working late again, David,' his wife's voice echoed softly in the room, tinged with concern but always understanding.

'Just finishing up some paperwork,' he replied without looking up, the sound of his pen scratching against paper filling the silence.

She walked over and gently took the pen from his hand. 'This can wait,' she insisted, her eyes locking on to his. 'You need a break. Let's go for a walk, just around the block. Some fresh air will do you good.'

David remembered how he had hesitated, the ever-present pull of responsibility tugging at him. But then he looked up into her eyes, saw the playful challenge there, and finally relented. 'Alright, but just around the block,' he had agreed, a reluctant smile breaking through. As they strolled through their neighborhood, her hand in his, David found himself relaxing for the first time that day. They talked about everything and nothing, her laughter a balm to his overworked mind. Coming home, she had teased him, 'See, the world didn't fall apart because Dr. Pace took a short break.' David had laughed, the sound mingling with hers, filling their home with warmth and light.

Returning to the present, David felt a pang in his heart. Those simple, spontaneous moments were what he missed the most. They were the reminders of a life filled with love and laughter, elements he had slowly let slip away in his grief. His fingertips grazed the smooth metal frame, a bittersweet echo of the feeling of her hand in his. It had been five years since he lost her, and the long battle with illness was finally over. He cherished their many happy years together, but the pain of her passing still lingered, a weight on his heart he doubted would ever fully lift. After she died, he threw himself wholly into his work, finding solace in helping others even as his personal world crumbled. David was the epitome of strength and reliability, or so his patients thought. *If only they saw me battling the TV remote every night*, he thought with a wry smile. In these quiet moments, the memories of their life together would return, more comforting than haunting. But at night, in the solitude of his home, memories of their life together would creep back in. He could still picture her standing at the stove, making breakfast on weekend mornings, sunlight streaming in through the kitchen windows. Sometimes he swore he could hear the echo of her laughter, like a ghost haunting the rooms they once shared. With a soft sigh, David neatly gathered the patient files on his desk and locked them away in the filing cabinet, keeping his busy mind focused on the tasks at hand. His schedule was packed again tomorrow, with an array of checkups and follow-ups, with a particularly challenging case in the afternoon. The variety of patients and their concerns kept his medical expertise sharp. David was known in the community for his competence, care, and uncanny ability to find every child's hidden 'brave button' during checkups. "Dr. Tickles strikes again," his patients' parents would often joke, appreciating his gentle approach.

After ensuring his desk was organized and his schedule was clear, David stood slowly, glancing around the office that often felt like a second home given the long hours he worked. He switched off the lamp atop the mahogany desk, casting the room into shadow.

Just as David was about to exit the clinic, his phone vibrated in his pocket, jolting him out of his reverie. Glancing at the caller ID, he recognized the number of one of his regular patients, Mrs. Henderson. Known for her spirited conversations and tendency to worry, she often called after hours for reassurance. With a sigh tinged with affectionate exasperation, David answered, "Good evening, Mrs. Henderson, what seems to be the matter this time?" The conversation that followed was a mix of medical queries and Mrs. Henderson's updates on her grandchildren's latest escapades. David listened patiently, offering advice with a gentle firmness. As he finally ended the call, a small smile played on his lips. *You're more than just a doctor to some of these folks*, he reminded himself, the brief interaction injecting a sense of purpose into his evening routine.

He made his way out of the building and into the parking lot. The sun was just beginning to dip below the horizon, signaling the end of another long but satisfying day. His sleek sedan purred to life as he turned the key in the ignition. It was a practical car, prioritizing function over flash, much like himself. As he navigated the streets of Claremont headed toward the upscale neighborhood of Bishopscourt, his thoughts began to wander. He contemplated his current situation—a successful doctor with an orderly, comfortable life, yet devoid of meaningful personal connections beyond his patients.

Occasionally, friends tried to gently push him back into the dating world, but he resisted. After experiencing such an intimate, loving marriage, the idea of casual dating held little appeal. The risk of deep loss again was too profound. As he waited at a light, watching pedestrians cross the street engaged in mundane tasks, he acknowledged that his reluctance toward relationships was born out of fear. Opening his heart again meant confronting that searing pain that accompanied love and loss. Yet David also sensed the creeping loneliness that permeated his days, despite his best efforts to stifle it with work and routine. There was an undeniable desire for companionship, for someone to share his inner world with. But any attempted connection thus far felt hollow, the ghost of his marriage forever lingering. The lights of the city blurred past as he continued driving, lost in thought. Would he spend the rest of his life clinging to the comfort of past memories rather than making room for new ones? He was too pragmatic for self-pity, yet being alone in the house they had shared wore him down in ways that he couldn't express. David contemplated the idea of selling the house, erasing those memories that haunted its walls. But the thought of leaving their home behind, the site of so much happiness, was too much to bear.

Turning onto his tree-lined street in Bishopscourt, David pushed aside his heavy thoughts as the sleek, modern lines of his house came into view. The landscaping was pristine, the greenery neatly manicured. His home was another reflection of his orderly nature and personal taste. As he pulled into the driveway, a feeling of comfort washed over him. However chaotic the world outside became, this was his sanctuary. Stepping inside, he immediately felt the silence embrace him. He took a moment to appreciate it after a day full of people and conversations. After slipping off his shoes, he moved smoothly through his nightly routine—showering to wash away the day, then preparing a simple but healthy meal for dinner. He avoided cooking elaborate spreads just for himself. A perfectly grilled piece of fish with fresh vegetables suited his practical nature. As he ate at the kitchen island, evening paper in hand, the emptiness of the house seemed more pronounced than usual. His wife had been the social one, always inviting people over for dinners or parties. The stillness now was at odds with the laughter and energy that used to fill these rooms. David glanced around the open-concept living space, meticulously decorated in a modern style and sparsely furnished with clean lines and neutral tones. He appreciated the tranquility but wondered if he had taken minimalism too far in his attempt to find a sense of calm. Perhaps the barren spaces reflected the emotional distance he maintained from most personal connections.

David tidied up the kitchen before retiring to his study, seeking comfort amidst the personal artifacts and leather-bound books that lined the shelves. He sank into his favorite leather chair beside the cold hearth, absently staring into the empty fireplace as he reflected on his day. His thoughts circled back to the café owner's suggestion to attend Friday's jazz night at Constantia Corner Café. At the time, David had given a noncommittal but polite response, as was his way. Crowds and small talk were hardly enticing to him. But perhaps viewing the invitation through a new lens would shift his perspective, stepping out of his regimented routine to partake in the community-offered connection, a counter to his pervasive isolation. The melody of live music and the quaint café ambiance might nourish his weary soul. He could view it as an experiment of sorts—a foray into new social situations instead of withdrawing further into the predictable safety of solitude. David realized that if he ever hoped to welcome new possibilities into his life, he needed to open himself to unfamiliar experiences that drew him out of his comfort zone.

With his decision made, he felt an unexpected glimmer of anticipation for the unknown possibilities the weekend could hold. The café's jazz night presented the perfect opportunity to gently immerse himself back into Cape Town's rich social tapestry he had neglected for too long. Though part of him reflexively recoiled at the prospect of small talk with strangers, a deeper intuition assured David that this was a step in the right direction. Perhaps mingling with some fellow jazz enthusiasts over coffee would reignite his dormant sense of adventure. The choice before him was clear: remain isolated in his grief or bravely reach out to embrace living again. With newfound resolve, he prepared for bed, comforted by the familiar routine. Moving through his well-practiced steps of brushing his teeth, changing into pajamas, and setting out clothes for tomorrow grounded him. Sliding between the cool Egyptian cotton sheets, David felt sleep quickly overtaking his exhausted mind and body.

But just as he drifted off, thoughts of Friday night's jazz presentation suddenly filled him with an unfamiliar nervous energy. What if he met someone interesting? His drowsy mind raced with possibilities that both thrilled and frightened his guarded heart. Turning restlessly in bed, David stared up at the ceiling fan as it circled in endless repetition. Sleep evaded him as he mentally composed introductory small talk and imagined meeting a woman who might understand his wounded but hopeful soul.

For the first time in years, the weekend held the promise of new beginnings instead of just more lonely hours to fill. The fan whirred steadily as David's eyes finally closed in anticipation of unknown possibilities.

Lisa

Lisa stood before her closet, her hand hovering over a deep-blue blouse. A flash of memory—the last disastrous date, the feeling of disappointment—flickered through her mind. Shaking it off, she chose the blouse, deciding tonight would be different. As she dressed, Lisa caught her reflection in the mirror. *Here's to new beginnings at this stage of life*, she thought, smiling at her own reflection. With a final approving glance in the mirror, Lisa's thoughts turned toward the evening ahead. The anticipation for the night was a refreshing change from her usual routine. As she drove to the café, her mind raced with conflicting thoughts. *Am I ready for this?* she wondered. She thought about the potential of the evening—the allure of jazz, the prospect of new connections. The familiar scents of the vine-covered valley wafted through the open car window, mingling with her sense of expectancy. Upon arriving at the Constantia Corner Café, the warm glow emanating from within seemed to echo her own budding excitement. Stepping out of her car, Lisa felt a rare surge of spontaneity, wondering what the night might hold.

Taking a deep breath, Lisa stepped inside. The café buzzed with the clink of glasses and the low hum of conversations. The aroma of rich coffee blended with the musty scent of old books and the rough texture of the wooden bookshelves added to the charm. The walls, adorned with vintage bookshelves, also boasted an eclectic collection of jazz memorabilia. Framed photographs of legendary jazz musicians, some autographed, whispered tales of the café's storied past. A saxophone, beautifully aged, hung near the small stage, almost as if awaiting a master's return. Each piece seemed to hold a story, resonating with Lisa's love for history. The tables, arranged intimately around the stage, drew patrons into the heart of the music. The space was more than a café; it was a sanctuary for those who cherished the rhythms of a bygone era. Lisa paused in the doorway, soaking in the ambiance. This neighborhood treasure had a character that mass-produced coffee shops lacked.

"Lisa! So glad you could make it."

She turned to see Jack approaching, his smile creasing the corners of his bright-blue eyes. He exuded a natural warmth that put her at ease.

"Thank you for the invite, Jack. I can already tell this will be a lovely evening."

"Well, we're happy to have you," Jack said. He leaned in conspiratorially. "I happen to know the best seat in the house if you're looking to get the full jazz experience."

Lisa glanced around. "Oh? And where might that be?"

"Follow me."

Jack wove through the scattered tables with familiar ease until they reached one near the small stage. A man Lisa recognized as a regular patron sat with his back to them, captivated by the music.

"Dr. Pace won't mind sharing," Jack said. "This is the primo spot for catching every soulful note. Enjoy!"

Before she could reply, Jack breezed back toward the counter, ever the dutiful host. Lisa stood uncertainly beside the table. The man turned his head, noticing her for the first time. His eyes crinkled as he smiled.

"Please, have a seat," he invited, his voice a pleasant baritone.

Lisa settled into the chair opposite him. "Thank you. I hope you don't mind me joining your table. Jack insisted this was the best view of the stage."

The man gave an easy chuckle. "Not at all. Can't argue with Jack's expertise." He extended his hand. "I'm David."

"Lisa." She returned his firm handshake. Up close, she noticed flecks of gray at his temples that lent an air of distinction. His brown eyes were sharp yet somehow sad.

"So," David began after a sip of coffee, "are you a local or just stopping in?"

Lisa found herself easing into the conversation with David, their mutual love of jazz sparking an immediate connection. "It's fascinating how jazz has evolved," she commented. "From classic roots to modern interpretations, it's like a reflection of our society's changes, don't you think?"

David nodded thoughtfully. "Absolutely. It mirrors the diversity and complexity of our times. Like that recent fusion project blending jazz with indigenous music—a beautiful example of cultural integration."

Lisa was pleasantly surprised. "I've been trying to bring a similar ethos into my boutique, incorporating sustainable fashion and local artisan work. It's about staying connected to the community and our environment."

Their discussion branched out, touching on themes of sustainability and cultural diversity. David shared his experiences with community projects, and Lisa talked about her efforts to support local artisans. It was more than shared interests; it was a shared perspective on engaging with the world around them.

Their mutual appreciation for jazz opened doors to shared memories and Lisa noticed a shadow cross David's face when he mentioned a particular jazz festival. It was fleeting, yet spoke volumes of a past perhaps not entirely at peace. As David spoke, Lisa noticed the depth in his voice that hinted at stories untold, a life rich with experiences and perhaps, like her own, tinged with its share of regrets and sorrow. In turn, Lisa found herself opening up about her boutique in Newlands, not just as a business venture but as a dream realized later in life, a testament to her resilience after her divorce. Each story shared was a window into their pasts, revealing the layers beneath their present selves.

When the band began a new, soulful piece, David and Lisa fell into an appreciative silence. The melody rose and fell like a living, breathing thing. Lisa closed her eyes, letting the rich sounds wash over her. At that moment, nothing else existed but the music's haunting beauty.

As the last vibrant note faded, Lisa opened her eyes with a contented sigh. "That was breathtaking," she said, turning to David. "Jazz always brings me back to simpler times," she remarked with a wistful smile. "It's like a balm for the soul, especially after a day in the bustling boutique."

David nodded, a reflective look crossing his face. "I know what you mean. Some pieces just speak to your soul. There's something about jazz… it understands the complexity of life, the sweet with the bitter." He paused, then added, "It's been a refuge for me, especially in the quieter moments of life."

Lisa sensed a shared understanding in his words, a hint at deeper currents beneath his calm exterior. She ventured, "It's funny how music can be both an escape and a way to face our truths, isn't it?"

Their gazes locked, lingering longer than necessary. Lisa felt a flutter in her stomach, a sensation she hadn't experienced in years. She saw a spark of something undefinable in David's eyes, mirroring her own mix of curiosity and attraction. She was acutely aware of his presence, the way his fingers tapped lightly to the rhythm of the music, the subtle warmth in his smile. The air around them seemed charged with an unspoken understanding, a tantalizing hint of possibilities. As the band struck up another lively number, the spell was momentarily broken. Yet, throughout the night, as they swayed subtly to the music and their conversation flowed effortlessly, Lisa found herself increasingly drawn to David. His laughter, his thoughtful nods, and every small gesture seemed to pull her closer. As closing time neared, a sense of reluctance washed over her. The thought of the evening ending, of parting ways with David, brought an unexpected twinge of disappointment.

"Thank you for sharing your table," she said. "I loved discovering this place."

David smiled warmly. "It was my pleasure. We should do this again sometime."

"I'd like that."

They exchanged numbers, both lingering longer than necessary before parting ways. Lisa stepped out into the night feeling lighter than she had in years. The music still resonated within her, mingling with thoughts of David.

During the drive home, Lisa marveled at the unexpected connection they had shared. She knew David was also emerging from heartbreak. They saw in each other a kindred spirit who understood loss but was open to new possibilities. For the first time since her divorce, Lisa felt a spark of excitement at the thought of getting to know someone—and being known.

By the time she arrived home, Lisa's cheeks ached from smiling. She fell asleep replaying moments from the evening and dreamed of jazz rhythms, brown eyes, and dark curls flecked with gray.

David

David arrived at Kirstenbosch Gardens, greeted by the fading sunlight that cast a golden glow over the greenery. He checked his watch—right on time. Glancing around, he felt a flutter of anticipation in his chest at the thought of seeing Lisa again. Since their encounter at the jazz café, he had found his thoughts constantly drifting back to her—her warm hazel eyes, her graceful elegance, the way she spoke with such passion. As he waited for Lisa, David found himself reflecting on the years gone by. The quiet of his home, once a haven, had become a reminder of solitude. He had grown accustomed to companionship in its simplest form, yet now, the prospect of something deeper stirred within him. It was a feeling he hadn't dared to entertain since his wife's passing. The apprehension was not just about opening his heart again, but about relearning the language of love at this stage in his life.

The crunch of gravel snapped David from his musings. He looked up to see Lisa walking toward him. The sun silhouetted her figure. She wore jeans and a crimson top, casual yet flattering. As she approached, David's pulse quickened.

"Lisa, so wonderful to see you again," he greeted warmly.

"Likewise," she replied with a smile. "Thank you for suggesting this. The gardens are breathtaking," Lisa remarked, her eyes taking in the scenery. "Though I must admit, I'm half expecting a mischievous gnome to pop out from behind one of these bushes." David chuckled, the image was amusing and oddly fitting amidst the lush greenery. As they began their walk, they exchanged light, easy banter. David pointed out a vibrant patch of wildflowers, and Lisa laughed about her not-so-green thumb. They discussed the weather, the scenic beauty of the gardens, and their favorite spots in the city. This casual conversation, sprinkled with laughter and shared observations, laid a comfortable groundwork for their burgeoning connection. In a rare moment of openness, David found himself sharing more about his past than he usually would.

"Being a general practitioner was more than a career; it was a calling," he explained, a reflective note in his voice. "There were challenging days, certainly, but the fulfillment of helping others... it's something that's stayed with me." He told Lisa of his rewarding yet demanding years as a general practitioner, drawn to the profession by his desire to help others. He spoke fondly of his late wife, the pain in his eyes belying the lightness of his tone. David found himself sharing more about his late wife than he had intended.

"She was vivacious, a perfect contrast to my stoicism," he explained. "And now, in these later years, I find that her spirit still guides me. It's taught me to seek joy, to be open to new experiences, even when they seem daunting."

Lisa listened intently, her eyes reflecting a deep understanding. It was clear she too had been shaped by her past, her experiences carving out a new path in her life after her divorce. "Some days, the grief is like an unexpected diagnosis—it hits hard and without warning," David said, his voice steady yet reflective. "In those moments, immersing myself in patient care isn't just a distraction, it's a balm. It helps me heal in small doses."

Lisa nodded, her expression reflective. "Staying busy is like stitching together a new pattern after everything's come undone. Post-divorce, my boutique wasn't just a shop; it was my canvas, a place where I could weave together new dreams and designs."

"It's true," David agreed pensively. "Sorrow has a way of realigning our priorities."

As they strolled beneath the leafy canopy, Lisa opened up about her journey since the divorce—how creating the boutique had been her lifeline, intertwining her passions for fashion and community. Her insightfulness and resilience stirred David's admiration. Lisa spoke of the years following her divorce, and the challenges of redefining her life on her own terms. "There's a certain strength you find in yourself," she mused, "when you're rebuilding your life later on. It's not just about starting over, but about rediscovering who you are now, at this point in your journey."

David nodded, feeling a kinship in their shared experience of transformation. It was a reminder that growth and change are constants, no matter one's age. The conversation meandered naturally to lighter topics—their shared love of gardening, amusing workplace anecdotes, and even debates over the best jazz musicians. Lisa's spirited humor coaxed David out of his usual solemn manner.

"You know, I used to think gardening was just about patience and a good watering can." David chuckled, brushing a leaf off his shoulder. "But there's an art to it, a science even."

"Absolutely," Lisa replied with a playful glint in her eye. "It's like coordinating an outfit—colors, textures, timing. It all has to come together just right."

The path wound its way through an array of exotic plants, each turn revealing a new natural wonder. It was here, amidst the quiet rustling of leaves and distant bird calls, that their conversation drifted, almost imperceptibly, from the casual to the personal. David commented on a particular flower, reminiscent of one his wife had adored. The mention seemed to hang in the air, a bridge to deeper, more intimate territories of conversation. They paused for a moment, looking at the flower. David felt Lisa's gaze on him, gentle and inquiring.

Her voice was soft when she spoke. "She must have been a remarkable person." Her words, though simple, reached deep within him, stirring memories. David once again found himself sharing more than he had intended, his voice tinged with a blend of nostalgia and acceptance. As he spoke, he could feel Lisa's empathetic presence beside him, her silent understanding lending him strength. In sharing his past, David felt a bridge forming between them, built on shared experiences and unspoken connections. In the stillness, David felt an intangible shift between them. Beyond the sights surrounding them, he was profoundly moved by the woman at his side. Her grace, her resilience, and the way she nurtured dreams once neglected stirred feelings long dormant within him. This profound connection with Lisa unlocked something deep inside that David had believed faded with the loss of his wife. He now sensed that the heart, like the earth, could be coaxed into blossoming again.

They continued along the path, both lost in their own reflections, closely attuned to each other's presence. Then, without warning, the skies opened up. Fat raindrops pelted down, eliciting cries of surprise. David spotted a large oak tree up ahead offering shelter.

"This way!" he called out, gently grasping Lisa's hand as they raced toward its canopy. They arrived breathless, raindrops glistening in Lisa's hair. She laughed brightly, her cheeks flushed with exhilaration. In the tree's sanctuary, surrounded by rustling leaves and the rain's steady cadence, they found themselves standing intimately close. David was intensely aware of her slender hand still enveloped in his.

David's heart raced as he looked at Lisa, raindrops glistening in her hair. A surge of emotions welled up within him—desire, hope, a hint of fear. It was a leap into the unknown, a step he hadn't taken in so long. As he tenderly caressed Lisa's cheek, he felt a connection that was more than physical; it was as if their souls were reaching out to each other. Her soft gasp as their eyes locked was all the encouragement he needed. When their lips met, it was like a gentle wave washing over him, soothing yet powerful. Her response was soft and yielding, a perfect harmony to his tentative approach. The kiss deepened, not just a mingling of lips but of hearts, a shared yearning for connection and understanding. As they embraced, the distant thunder seemed to echo the tumult of emotions within David. A mixture of exhilaration, relief, and a budding hope. As they slowly parted, David was left breathless, his mind a whirlwind of emotion. The kiss had been comforting, like coming home, yet thrilling in its promise of new beginnings. In that moment, he realized how profoundly he had yearned for this connection, how much he had missed the simple yet profound joy of sharing such intimacy. It was a revelation, a sweet awakening to possibilities he had thought were lost to him.

Lisa's eyes shone. "So... that was unexpected," she murmured.

David let out an apologetic chuckle. "I hope not unpleasantly so."

"No, not at all." Her tone was warm, yet he sensed the shadow of hesitation. "It's just... with my past, I'm wary of rushing into anything."

David nodded. "Of course. I understand. My wounds run deep as well." He drew in a steadying breath. "Perhaps we might explore this slowly? I care too much to risk causing either of us more hurt."

Lisa smiled, gratitude shining in her eyes. "I'd like that." She gave his hand a grateful squeeze. The rain had slowed to a drizzle, beads glistening on the leaves around them.

They set off again down the trail. As the afternoon faded into evening, their conversation flowed effortlessly—hopes and dreams interwoven with funny mishaps and poignant observations. The fresh, woodsy air seemed infused with promise. Too soon they arrived back at the gardens' entrance. An inviting bistro beckoned nearby, couples laughing over wine on its patio. David turned to Lisa, not yet ready for the evening to end.

"Would you care to join me for a bite?" he asked hopefully.

Lisa's eyes glinted with shared reluctance. "I wish I could, but I've got an early day tomorrow." She touched his arm lightly. "But perhaps later in the week?"

"It's a date," David smiled. They exchanged a brief but tender parting kiss. As Lisa drove off, David raised his hand in farewell, already counting the moments until he would see her again.

When David arrived home, he was greeted by silence. But it wasn't the heavy, lonely silence he was accustomed to. Tonight it felt like the tranquil hush of new beginnings, rife with possibility. He prepared for bed slowly, still caught in the glow of the evening. Sliding under cool sheets, sleep found David quickly. His dreams were sweet, painted in dusky sunsets, chestnut hair, and tender raindrop kisses.

Lisa

Morning sunlight streamed through the windows of Lisa's cozy Rondebosch cottage, stirring her from sleep. As her eyes fluttered open, memories of last evening flooded back in a rush. David's tender smile, their intimate conversation, the soft patter of rain on leaves... and that kiss. Lisa's fingers traced her lips, tingling as she recalled the exquisite sensation of David's kiss. It was a symphony of warmth and electricity, gentle yet impassioned that awakened a longing she hadn't known she was capable of. The memory of his lips, soft yet assertive against hers, lingered in her mind, stirring a fusion of comfort and exhilaration. It was like the first bloom of spring after a long winter—both refreshing and deeply familiar, awakening a sense of coming home to a place she hadn't yet discovered.

As the morning light filtered through the window, Lisa acknowledged her deepening feelings for David, a realization that came as both a surprise and a concern. She pondered the implications of starting a new relationship so soon after her divorce, a thought that brought a mix of excitement and apprehension. With a sigh, Lisa slid out from under the covers and padded to the kitchen. Leaning against the counter as the coffee brewed, Lisa found the familiar, comforting aroma of coffee fading into the background. Her thoughts were preoccupied, not with doubts, but with the practicalities of what a new relationship entailed.

Her mind briefly touched upon her past marriage, once a beacon of hope, now a reminder of what she sought to avoid. Over the years, her ex-husband had grown more distant, absorbed in his work. Their once effortless connection had slowly withered like an untended garden. The emotional neglect had left Lisa wary, afraid to bare her soul, only to be met with apathy again. The shrill beep of the coffee maker jolted Lisa back to the present. As she poured a cup, her eyes landed on a vase of fresh dahlias she had bought just yesterday. Their bright, bold petals reminded her of her kiss with David—vivid and exhilarating. Lisa smiled softly, remembering the way he had looked at her with such tenderness. It had made her feel truly seen. Maybe she owed it to herself to nurture this new connection, even if it felt risky. After all, her boutique had started as just a dream, and now it was a thriving reality. With care and patience, dreams could blossom into something beautiful.

As she tidied up the kitchen, Lisa's gaze fell on a framed photo of herself and her ex on their wedding day, their youthful smiles brimming with hope. She studied it for a moment, marveling at how much could change in the space between those captured moments. With time, the foundation of any relationship could subtly shift and crack if not tended to. She wondered—did she have the energy to pour herself wholly into something new? And what if she offered her bruised heart, only to have it handled carelessly again?

On impulse, Lisa grabbed her phone and dialed her best friend, Amanda. The line clicked as her bubbly voice filled the speaker.

"Lisa! How's my favorite fashion queen?"

Lisa laughed. "Still reigning, stronger than ever. Amanda, I need your insight on something." After briefly updating Amanda on the developments with David, her tone mixed with a hint of irony. "It's like I'm in a romance novel, but I skipped the chapter on how to deal with post-kiss jitters." Lisa's tone shifted, revealing vulnerability. "Amanda, I'm at a crossroads here. I feel this deep, undeniable connection with David, something I haven't felt in... I can't even remember how long. Yet, there's this voice inside me, scared of repeating past mistakes."

Amanda made a sympathetic noise. "Oh, honey, it sounds like you've really connected with David. It's natural to be cautious, especially after everything with the Ex from Hell." After a thoughtful pause, she added gently, "You're not the same person you were back then, Lisa. You've grown so much. And you deserve to find someone who cherishes that." Amanda's voice was warm and reassuring. "It's natural to feel cautious but don't let fear hold you back. You're stronger now, Lisa. And you deserve to find happiness."

Lisa smiled slightly, Amanda's optimism dulling her doubts. "Exactly. I've changed, haven't I? And maybe it's time my choices reflect that growth. It's not about diving headfirst into the unknown, but about stepping forward with open eyes and an open heart. I just needed to hear it from someone else, too." They chatted a bit longer before Lisa had to start getting ready for work. She hung up feeling lighter, resolving to take things one day at a time.

Arriving at her boutique, Lisa immersed herself in the morning tasks, her thoughts intermittently drifting to David. While meticulously arranging a new display of handmade scarves, she was interrupted by the chime of the door. A regular customer, Mrs. Jenkins, stepped in, her eyes immediately drawn to the vibrant scarves.

"Lisa, these are just divine! Are they new?" Mrs. Jenkins asked, her enthusiasm infectious.

"Yes, they just arrived. Handmade right here in Cape Town," Lisa replied, her spirits lifted by the interaction.

As Mrs. Jenkins carefully examined each scarf, her admiration reminding Lisa of the pride she took in her work, a parallel struck her. The way she nurtured her boutique, selecting each item with care and thought, mirrored how she wanted to approach her budding relationship with David—with mindfulness and dedication. This realization brought a soft smile to her face, easing some of the morning's heaviness. In this newfound lightness, Lisa's gaze wandered over the familiar corners of her boutique, her heart swelling with a sense of accomplishment. It was this very sense of fulfillment and independence she brought into every aspect of her life, she realized. Tucking away these reflections, she decided it was time for a break, a moment to step away and perhaps gain a new perspective on things.

After Mrs. Jenkins left with her purchase, Lisa's attention was captured by a notification on her boutique's social media page. A recent post showcasing her unique, ethically sourced scarf collection garnered unexpected attention, including a repost from a popular eco-conscious fashion influencer. Surprised and invigorated by this sudden spotlight, Lisa felt a surge of pride and excitement. Her commitment to sustainable fashion was not just a business decision but a personal passion, and seeing it resonate with a wider audience brought a new dimension to her day. The buzz around her post also sparked a reflection on her personal life. Just as she was embracing modern approaches in her business, she wondered if she could apply a similar mindset to her relationships. Maybe her connection with David was not about revisiting the past but about embracing a future.

With this thought, Lisa felt a renewed sense of purpose, both in her professional life and in her contemplations about David. Realizing how quickly the morning had passed, she felt a pang of hunger. Her reflections, coupled with the steady flow of customers, had left her feeling a bit drained. *A break would do me good*, she thought, tidying up the counter. The boutique was calm for the moment, a perfect opportunity for a quick lunch. Lisa closed the door of her boutique behind her and made her way to the nearby café. The short walk there allowed her to enjoy the gentle warmth of the midday sun and the bustling energy of the street, a stark contrast to the quiet of her shop. As she arrived at the café, already filled with the lunchtime crowd, she found a spot in line. The change of environment was a welcome distraction. As she waited in line to order, she heard a familiar voice call her name. Turning, she broke into a smile as she recognized one of her old college friends, Mara. After quick hugs and promises to catch up properly soon, Mara revealed some news. She had recently gotten engaged to a wonderful man she met at a friend's dinner party.

"I was so afraid to open my heart again after my divorce," Mara confessed. "But taking that leap of faith with Colin was the best decision I ever made."

Lisa was struck by her friend's story, sensing the parallel to her own crossroads with David. She realized that bravely embracing new chapters, despite past hurt, could lead to beautiful outcomes. After parting ways with renewed enthusiasm to reunite soon, Lisa felt buoyed by the encounter. She spent the remainder of the afternoon at the boutique feeling markedly lighter. The nervous flutters she had felt that morning seemed to have settled into a gentle anticipation.

The afternoon passed quickly in a flurry of customers. Before she knew it, it was closing time. Lisa tidied up, then locked the front door behind her, breathing in the crisp evening air. As she climbed into her car, dusk was falling, bathing the streets in hazy violet light. Impulsively, she decided to take the scenic route home through the neighborhoods instead of the main roads. A walk might help clear her head. The gravel paths of Rondebosch were tranquil compared to Newlands' bustling commerce. Lisa strolled past rows of trees and Victorian-style homes, most with lamps already aglow in their windows. The fresh air and exercise unknotted the tension of the day.

Matching her breaths to her slow footsteps, Lisa's thoughts revolved around one central question—should she allow this new connection with David to develop or protect her still-mending heart? She replayed every nuance of their interactions, searching for clues. Had she imagined that spark between them? Was she misreading simple chemistry as a deeper bond? No, her instincts told her. What they shared transcended physical attraction. The understanding in David's eyes when she revealed glimpses of her past heartaches and rebuilt dreams... that came from a place of empathy, of seeing her wholly. She felt certain he would treat the blossoming trust between them as delicately as the rain-drenched petals of a rose. And hadn't she spent too long closed off in fear, denying herself connection? If she was ever going to welcome love again, she owed it to herself to take this chance with eyes wide open. By the time Lisa arrived back home, twilight had faded to an inky night. She stepped into the circle of light on her front porch, fishing for the keys in her handbag. Inside at last, she leaned back against the closed door and let out a long breath she hadn't realized she'd been holding.

The choices stretched out before her were suddenly clear. She would talk to David openly about her worries, giving this relationship a chance while proceeding mindfully. They would get to know each other, flaws and all, navigating life's unpredictable waters together. Lisa smiled softly, imagining quiet conversations curled up in each other's arms. The terrifying precipice of potential heartbreak was still there. But so too was the promise of true partnership and being fully seen. With her decision made, Lisa felt emboldened to face her fears. She brewed a cup of chamomile tea and settled on the couch, rehearsing what she would tell David about her past and their possible future.

Suddenly, her cell phone rang, jolting Lisa from her thoughts. She glanced at the screen. Speak of the devil—it was David calling.

With a deep breath, she answered. "Hello, David..."

David

David stood in his spacious modern kitchen, his hand pausing over the dish towel. A flicker of doubt shadowed his thoughts. Was he moving too fast with Lisa? He shook his head, trying to dispel the worry, but it clung to him, a whisper of fear amidst his anticipation as he checked on the bobotie baking in the oven. The aroma of warming spices filled the room, mingling with the fresh flowers he had placed on the dining table. In just over an hour, Lisa would be here, in his home.

David's mind drifted back over the past few weeks spent getting to know Lisa. He treasured the memories of their explorations of Cape Town. Strolling through Kirstenbosch Gardens, discovering colorful booths at the Oranjezicht farmer's market, laughing over coffee at sidewalk cafés in Seapoint. Each new experience with Lisa was like a brushstroke, slowly filling in the landscape of this unexpected relationship. Every glimpse he caught of her smile, every twinkle in her hazel eyes, drew him deeper under her spell. David chuckled as he recalled their debate over the best coffee shops in the city. Lisa had argued passionately for the Truth Coffee Roasting, while David remained loyal to the Constantia Corner Café's rich brews.

"We may have to agree to disagree on this," Lisa had finally said, laughing. "But I suppose there are benefits to finding new favorites together." The fond memory now brought a rush of affection. No longer just passing acquaintances, they were crafting shared experiences, shared tastes, and shared lives.

Tonight felt different though. More significant. He wanted to create not just a pleasant dinner but an evening filled with warmth, laughter, and rich conversation. An experience they would hold dear in the days to come. David inspected his homemade bobotie, pleased with the blend of flavors—savory minced meat and onions in a baked custard, topped with a dash of chutney. He knew Lisa enjoyed bold spices from their conversations about travel and food. This traditional dish felt personal, a meal to nourish the heart as much as the body.

Glancing at his watch, David wiped his hands on a dish towel and hurried to change into a crisp blue shirt and khaki pants. He tousled his dark curls, flecked with gray, and inspected his reflection. The lines etched around his brown eyes spoke of a lifetime of laughter and sorrow. But tonight, joy shone in his expression, a lightness he hadn't felt in years.

David's pulse quickened at the sound of the doorbell. With a deep breath, he went to let Lisa in. As the door swung open, his breath caught at the vision before him. Lisa looked radiant in a flowing purple dress that accentuated her graceful frame. Her chestnut waves were swept over one shoulder, and her hazel eyes gleamed with a warmth that melted his heart. Suddenly, words escaped him.

Lisa broke the silence first, gifting him that coy smile that made his knees weak. "Good evening, David. Thank you for having me over."

David collected himself and smiled back. "The pleasure is all mine. Please, come in."

He led her into the dining room, pulling out a chair for her. "You look beautiful tonight," he said sincerely. Lisa's eyes crinkled as she thanked him. *Yes*, David thought, *this felt right*. No longer two solitary souls but a union glowing with new promise.

As the conversation over dinner progressed, David, lost in the comfort of their banter, casually mentioned a jazz club he used to frequent with his late wife. He noticed a shift in Lisa's demeanor, her smile dimming slightly.

"I hope I'm not just a replacement for memories," she said, her voice a soft whisper, revealing an unexpected vulnerability.

David's heart clenched at her words. Had he been too caught up in his nostalgia? "No, Lisa, that's not it at all," he hurried to reassure her, his voice earnest. "You're not a replacement. You're a wonderful new chapter in my life. I'm sorry if I made you feel otherwise." He reached across the table, offering a gentle touch of apology. Lisa's eyes searched his, then slowly, her smile returned, a little wiser, a little more trusting. Lisa nodded, a hint of relief in her gaze. "I guess every good jazz tune has minor notes," she quipped, lightening the mood. David laughed, the tension dissipating between them.

"And every good meal has its sweet dessert," he said, rising to bring out the Malva pudding he had prepared. As they indulged in the dessert, their conversation shifted to lighter topics. They traded playful jibes about their favorite authors, the laughter and ease returning, reaffirming the unique connection they shared. "The gardens in Kirstenbosch were so rejuvenating," Lisa remarked. "Remember how we got caught in that sudden rainstorm?" She smiled, a playful glint in her eyes.

David chuckled at the memory. "And we raced for cover under that big oak tree. I've never been so drenched!" He paused, then added more solemnly, "But I'll never forget how beautiful you looked with raindrops in your hair."

Lisa blushed charmingly. "Neither will I forget our first kiss. It felt like a dream."

They reminisced fondly over every park stroll, museum tour, and jazz performance attended, reminiscing over the journey that had led them here. Around them, the dining room glowed warmly under the soft candlelight, casting shadows that danced along the walls. The rich aroma of bobotie mingled with the subtle scent of the red wine, enhancing the coziness of the evening. Their conversation lingered, speaking of hopes more than past sorrows. David even shared his idea of renovating his backyard to include a small botanical garden.

"It would be such a peaceful place to read or have coffee on nice mornings," he said. "I'd love to create something nurturing and vibrant." Lisa's eyes lit up, a trace of nostalgia in her voice. "That reminds me of the small garden my grandparents had. I used to help them every weekend. I could see us out there planning the landscaping." She sighed contentedly. "Tonight has been perfect, David."

After dinner, as they washed the dishes, David broached the earlier topic. "Lisa, I want you to know that my memories don't diminish what I feel for you. They're part of who I am, but with you, I'm discovering new joys."

Lisa listened, her expression softening. "I appreciate you sharing that, David. I'm not here to replace anyone; I'm here because what we have is special."

Rinsing a wineglass, David stole a glance at her graceful profile. A warm contentment glowed inside him. He could get used to this. Sharing the little moments that comprised a life together.

In the living room, David and Lisa sat closely on the couch, limbs entwined. The lamps cast a soft glow as music played gently in the background.

Lisa traced her fingertip lightly across David's jaw. "You've made me feel so cared for tonight," she murmured.

David caressed her cheek, his gaze lost in the depth of her hazel eyes. "You deserve nothing less," he whispered. Gently, he drew her close, their lips meeting in a tender, lingering kiss. It was a kiss that spoke more of promise than of passion, a gentle affirmation of their growing feelings. Lisa leaned into his embrace. In the quiet of the living room, their closeness was more emotional than physical. Their hands entwined, they shared glances and smiles, each touch and look weaving a deeper bond of understanding and affection. As the evening deepened, they found themselves drawn closer, their conversation a tapestry of shared memories and unspoken promises. Wordlessly, David took her hand, leading her to his bedroom and the promise of intimate connection. They came together in a perfect harmony of affection, longing, and tentative joy, emotions laid bare in their tender exploration.

Later, as the night deepened, Lisa stirred, offering a tender smile before drifting back to sleep. David lay awake, marveling not at the physical closeness but at the emotional bond they had strengthened. Her presence filled him with a sense of peace and belonging. A fierce protectiveness welled up in him, coupled with a profound sense of awe that they had found each other. He placed the softest kiss on her bare shoulder. As she smiled in her sleep, he knew then that he was falling in love with this remarkable woman who had reignited forgotten parts of his soul. The revelation delivered a bittersweet ache—indescribable joy twined with the haunting fear of loss.

In the darkest hours before dawn, David lay awake, a tumult of emotions swirling within him. His fear of losing Lisa battled with his desire to fully embrace their relationship. He knew he had to let go of his past apprehensions to offer Lisa the love she deserved. With a featherlight touch, he traced her shoulder, still hardly daring to believe they had found each other. She stirred slightly with a contented sigh that flooded David with fierce tenderness. In these quiet moments, he confronted the past he still clung to and the daunting future he now dared to envision.

After Lisa had left in the gentle light of morning, David stood at the window, watching until her car disappeared from view. Lisa's absence after their intimacy felt jarring, leaving an almost physical ache. He wandered back to the bedroom they had filled with passion, now silent once more. A bittersweet revelation permeated David's thoughts. He wanted Lisa always by his side, to build a life with her. The realization both thrilled and terrified him. Since losing his wife, he had sealed his heart away to protect it from further pain. But Lisa had slipped past his defenses with her warmth and wisdom. The thought of losing her love was too much to bear.

David sank onto the bed where Lisa had been curled against him just moments before. Her scent still lingered in the cushions. He ached to hold her again, to confess the love overflowing in his heart. But the familiar demons of fear and doubt crept in, reminding David of the steep price that accompanied such profound love. With a heavy sigh, he leaned forward, elbows on his knees and head in hands.

Images from the evening replayed in his mind. Lisa's dazzling smile, the candlelight dancing in her eyes, her head nestled trustingly against his chest. The memories centered David, grounding him in the present even as his old wounds cried out. This was no time for past regrets and future worries. He and Lisa had crafted something beautiful, a love both nurturing and exhilarating. He could cling to past heartache, or boldly walk forward into Lisa's outstretched arms.

As David prepared for the day, he resolved to welcome love anew in all its tender magnificence. David knew he was ready to embrace whatever future lay ahead with Lisa. With her by his side, he could conquer anything, even his lingering doubts. This time, he would savor each moment as the gift it was.

Lisa

Lisa sighed, watching the sun set from her boutique window. The day's rush had ebbed to a calm, leaving a handful of customers. She appreciated this slower rhythm after the energetic commotion of her busy shop. It granted her a moment of stillness for reflection before closing up for the evening.

While rearranging handcrafted bracelets, Lisa's mind drifted to David. She smiled, recalling their laughter under Kirstenbosch's rain-soaked trees and last night's romantic dinner, but her smile faded as uncertainty crept in. Were they moving too fast? Was she ready to fully intertwine her life with another's after only recently reclaiming her independence?

The jingle of the bell above the door pulled Lisa back from her reverie. As she glanced up, her heart skipped a beat, not from excitement but a familiar dread. Richard, her ex-husband, stepped into the boutique, unwittingly bringing a shadow of her past with him. While his appearance stirred old memories, Lisa reminded herself of the strength she had found since those days. "Richard... I wasn't expecting to see you," Lisa said, struggling to keep her tone light despite the discomfort twisting in her stomach. "What brings you by?"

Richard scanned the boutique, his tone casual but eyes sharp. "Thought I'd check on your little project," he said, the word *little* lingering like a taunt.

His condescending tone sent a cold prickle racing up Lisa's spine, her fingers curling into her palm. She steadied herself against the counter, her smile strained but polite. "As you can see, I am doing quite well," she managed to say, despite the slight quiver in her voice.

"Glad to hear it," Richard replied absently, already looking away. He watched the remaining customers for a moment before turning back to Lisa. "I saw you the other night, you know. At that café over in Constantia." His gaze was probing. "With a gentleman friend."

Richard's words ignited a spark of anger in Lisa. She clenched her fists, hidden behind her back, as memories of their suffocating marriage flashed in her mind. She focused on a bracelet on the counter, its beads cool under her touch, a contrast to the heat of her rising ire. Striving to keep her voice steady, she replied, "I don't see how that's any of your concern, Richard."

He held up his hands innocently. "Hey, no judgment here. I'm happy you're moving on. Rebound relationships can be tricky though." His words were patronizing. Before she could respond, he continued lightly. "Wouldn't want you rushing into anything too quickly, getting your heart broken all over again."

Upon Richard's probing, Lisa felt a knot of discomfort tighten in her stomach. She masked her growing unease with a measured response. "I don't see how that's any of your concern, Richard." Her voice was calm, but inside, a storm of emotions began to brew, each word from Richard adding to her rising tide of anxiety.

A smirk tugged at Richard's lips, sending Lisa's heart into an uneasy dance. It was a familiar expression, one that brought back a flood of unpleasant memories. She felt a lump forming in her throat as he nonchalantly glanced at his watch. "Of course, you know I just want you to be careful," he said, before adding with a wink, "Yikes, gotta run."

As he sauntered out, Lisa's grip on the counter loosened, her body simultaneously relaxing and trembling with the aftershocks of his presence. She exhaled slowly, her fingers gradually uncurling from the tight fists she hadn't even realized she'd made. Richard's visit had stirred a familiar turmoil within her, an unwelcome intrusion that lingered even after he left. She attempted to refocus on her closing tasks, but his words echoed in her mind, their sharp edges gently poking at her newfound peace. She found herself questioning every smile, every touch shared with David. Were they truly moving forward or merely escaping their pasts? The more she pondered, the more Richard's insinuations seemed to hold a bitter truth. Her heart ached at the thought, a deep, gnawing fear taking root. Was she diving headfirst into a new relationship without fully healing from the old? She locked the boutique door, her thoughts a turbulent storm as she headed to meet David.

The drive to the Constantia Corner Café seemed longer than usual, each turn and stoplight giving Lisa more time to deliberate. Her mind was a whirlpool of conflicting emotions, her grip on the steering wheel tightening and loosening as she navigated both the road and her tangled thoughts. By the time she parked, her heart was racing, a tumultuous blend of fear and uncertainty clouding her thoughts. As she sat across from David, her smile was strained, the shadows of her inner turmoil dimming its brightness. His familiar, comforting presence, which usually calmed her, now seemed like a beacon for her fears to converge upon. They exchanged pleasantries, but Lisa only picked at her food, her appetite diminished by gnawing anxiety. When David remarked fondly on a painting his late wife had loved, Lisa felt something inside her snap. Richard's warning echoed in her mind, heightening her insecurity.

"Am I just a substitute for your wife?" Lisa's voice trembled with a mix of accusation and fear.

David's face registered shock, his words coming slower, laced with disbelief. "What? No, Lisa... why... why would you even think something like that?"

Dinner with David became a battlefield of Lisa's emotions. His every word, once comforting, now echoed with doubts seeded by Richard's insinuations. Finally, unable to contain the tumult inside, her words spilled out, tinged with a desperation she hardly recognized. "I feel like I'm competing with a ghost sometimes," she admitted, her voice quivering with a mix of fear and confusion. "Like I'll never measure up to your memories."

David reached for her hand, his eyes filled with concern. "Lisa, listen, you could never be just a substitute to me. You're your own vibrant soul. You have to know that."

"How can I be sure," Lisa's voice wavered, "when memories of her seem to linger everywhere? Like with the painting..." She paused, her voice softening, not out of calm but an overwhelming sense of vulnerability. "It makes me wonder where I fit into all this."

David's response came slower, his voice tinged with a mixture of hurt and confusion. "Lisa, that... that's not fair. I... I cherish my past, yes, but that doesn't mean I don't care about you, about us." His defensive tone only heightened Lisa's agitation. Richard's smug face flashed in her mind. "Right, silly me for wanting more than to just be some feel-good fling for you!"

David looked shocked. "You know that's not true. Why are you twisting this?"

Lisa pressed her fingertips to her temples, a gesture more of frustration than fatigue. Her eyes briefly closed as she gathered her scattered thoughts. This was all too familiar—misreading signals, choking down feelings. It brought back visceral memories of her marriage disintegrating into polite distance. She had sworn never to swallow her doubts again, yet here she was, questioning herself and silencing her voice.

"I can't do this," Lisa's voice broke. "I won't relive the shadows of a past relationship. I can't be second to memories. It's too painful."

David reached out a placating hand. "Let's just take a breath and talk this through." But Lisa recoiled from his touch, the gulf between them suddenly feeling insurmountable.

"I have talked. You're not hearing me." She looked at him sadly. "I can't be with someone who makes me feel invisible."

Before David could respond, Lisa grabbed her purse and hurried out, desperate to escape the cloying grip of past hurts threatening to swallow her whole. His voice calling her name trailed off as the café door swung shut behind her.

The night air was bracing, anchoring Lisa as she walked quickly through the parking lot to her car. She just needed to get away, to quiet the storm raging inside her. Had she overreacted? She wanted to believe David's reassurances, but the rawness of old wounds made it impossible to think clearly. Better to protect herself now than repeat the agonizing descent into emotional isolation.

By the time Lisa arrived home, she felt drained and emotionally hollowed out. She drifted through her nightly routine in a daze, replaying the heated words at the café. Each time David's voice echoed in her mind, a fresh wave of sadness washed over her, leaving her raw. She cared for him deeply, but the scars of the past ran too deep. As she crawled between the cool sheets, Lisa braced herself for a restless night.

Sleep evaded her for hours as she agonized over whether ending things with David had been rash. Moonlight filtered through the curtains as she lay staring up at the ceiling fan's repetitive path, around and around. She traced its circling path with her eyes, trying to halt her racing mind. Had walking out been a cowardly retreat or an act of self-preservation? Lisa squeezed her eyes shut against the doubts barraging her. She couldn't risk her newly mended heart, not even for David. Better to retreat behind walls than expose herself to harm again.

Exhaustion finally granted her a few fitful hours of sleep. But too soon, pale dawn light stirred her awake. The argument came flooding back like a forgotten bad dream. Lisa sat up slowly, hugging her knees to her chest. The soft morning sun revealed no magical solutions, only the knowledge that some wounds run too deep to be easily soothed. However much she cared for David, she could not simply trust again so unconditionally. Not after years of neglect that had left her insecure and wary. No, as painful as it was, ending things last night was the right choice. She could not withstand feeling doubt so acute again.

"Alone," she whispered into the silence of her room, a single tear tracing her cheek as she faced the haunting realization that solitude might be her only refuge from heartache. After a quick shower, Lisa dressed for work, bracing herself to face the day. She focused on practicalities. Opening the boutique, assisting customers, placing orders, and allowing the familiar tasks to ground her. If she kept busy, she could keep heartbreak at bay.

The jangling bell announced her first customer shortly after opening. Lisa straightened up, swallowing down the sadness that gripped her throat, and forced a polite smile. "Good morning! Let me know if you need any help." The customer nodded happily and went back to browsing. Lisa let out a breath.

She could do this. Push past the ache and continue living, just as she had survived before. For now, she would immerse herself in work and try not to imagine David's face.

David

David lay awake, feeling the void Lisa's absence left. Each clock tick amplified a stark realization. His world was incomplete without her. It wasn't just her absence; it was the absence of a future he'd only just begun to envision with her. Sleep evaded him, thoughts of their last conversation echoing through the dark hours. The look in her eyes as she fled the café haunted him—confusion and fear swirling with hurt. He glanced at the clock's red glow. It was 2:37 a.m. With a resigned sigh, he threw off the covers and sat on the edge of the bed.

He raked a hand through his gray-flecked curls. How had everything crumbled so quickly? One minute they were blissfully planning his future garden, the next arguing over ghosts from the past. Her pained words sank hooks into his heart. She felt invisible, competing with his late wife's memory. The accusation stunned David, shaking him from his contented reverie. Of course, he still held his past dear, but Lisa had awakened new parts of his soul. Didn't she realize she was her own radiant fire, never just a substitute glow?

At the window, David faced the night's chill, contrasting his fevered thoughts. The moonlight laid bare his emotions. He pushed the curtains aside, revealing a waxing moon suspended in inky dusk. Its pearly light illuminated the empty streets with an ethereal glow. David pressed his fingertips to the cool glass, aching for the warmth of Lisa's touch. How had he allowed this distance to grow between them? He should have been more sensitive to her doubts and reassured her of his feelings. But the shock of her words had rendered him speechless, unable to convey the depths of his heart.

As the first light of dawn crept into the sky, a restless David abandoned the idea of sleep. In the kitchen, while preparing tea, his every movement was an echo of introspection. While the water heated, so did the realization that his next actions could mend or end everything. His heart knew the answer, even as his mind wrestled with the gravity of it. He checked his phone again. Still no response from Lisa. His calls and texts had gone unanswered, leaving a hollow pit in his stomach. Had she written him off completely? The very thought made David's chest constrict. The thought of losing her, especially like this, sent a wave of panic crashing over him.

Palms braced on the counter, head bowed, David exhaled slowly until the kettle's shrill whistle broke the silence. Steeping his tea, an impulse gripped him. He had to do something grand, romantic, to show Lisa what she meant to him. Prove this was more than a fling or escape from the past. He rummaged through the junk drawer until he found a notepad and pen. Perched on a stool, David began to scribble ideas, exhilaration and fear blending as a plan took shape. He would recreate their first magical night and remind Lisa of the undeniable connection between them. Candlelight, music, and an intimate garden transformed under twinkling fairy lights. Their story wouldn't end here, not if he could help it.

As David wrestled with a stubborn string of fairy lights that seemed to have a life of its own, he couldn't help but chuckle. "Supposed to be creating romance, not a knotted mess," he muttered to himself. The lights, finally untangled and draped elegantly, seemed to twinkle as if in triumph. Each candle and each string of lights was more than decoration; they were symbols of renewal and hope. The space glowed under the soft lights woven through branches and foliage. In the planter boxes along the fence, tall taper candles flickered, their flames dancing in the gentle breeze. A small table set for two held a bouquet of wildflowers, their fragrance sweetening the air. *It is straight from a romance novel*, David mused. He hoped it would speak to Lisa's heart and remind her of their irreplaceable bond.

As afternoon faded to dusk, David paced the patio, pulsating with nervous energy. In his pocket, his phone remained silent, punctuating the passing minutes. He glanced at his watch again. Six forty-five p.m. If he had estimated correctly, Lisa would be home soon. While setting up the music, David tried humming along to a tune, only to realize he was completely off-key. "Good thing I hired a professional." He chuckled, sending a quick text to confirm with the sax player. *All set up across the street. Let me know when you're ready.* David typed a quick reply, thanking him.

He took a steadying breath, picturing Lisa arriving home. In his mind, he rehearsed what he would say, how he would bare his soul and plead for a second chance. But words suddenly felt insufficient for the depth of his feelings. He would speak from the heart and trust the rest to fate. The faint noise of an approaching engine snapped David's attention to the street. Headlights flashed across the hedges as Lisa's car turned into her driveway. It was time.

As Lisa arrived, the air seemed to hold its breath. David watched from the shadows, his heart in his throat. He saw her hesitate, her body language a mix of surprise and caution. He could almost hear her thoughts, the internal debate whether to open her heart or guard it. He felt a surge of longing to reach out, to ease her fears. Her expression, caught between surprise and hesitation, sent a pang of doubt through him. Had his efforts only deepened her uncertainty?

The candle flames cast a warm glow across her face as she slowly approached the garden gate. She took in the lights, flowers, and table set for two, the hint of a smile ghosting her lips. At that moment, the sax player began a soulful, yearning melody from his spot across the street. The soundtrack for David's emotional plea. Her searching gaze, landing on him as he stepped forward, seemed to question the intention behind his grand arrangement.

"David... what is all this?" Lisa asked, her voice barely audible above the music.

David's voice barely rose above a whisper, each word trembling with sincerity. "All this? It's my heart, Lisa, trying to reach yours. A gesture, perhaps small, but for something far bigger that I feel for you." He took a hesitant step toward her, his voice a fragile blend of hope and apprehension. "Lisa, this might seem overwhelming... but it's the truest expression of what I feel for you." He stopped before her, the gulf between them feeling suddenly insurmountable. He searched her eyes, seeing traces of the same fractured hurt he too had carried for so long.

"Lisa..." David took a hesitant step forward. "I won't pretend my past isn't a part of me, but it doesn't define what I feel for you, what we could build together. You've brought light into corners of my heart I thought were forever dimmed." He hesitantly reached for her hand. She didn't pull away. David felt a spark of hope.

"I've carried grief with me for many years," he confessed. "But you've awakened something unexpectedly beautiful. What I feel for you, it's because of who you are, Lisa. Your grace, your wisdom. Not faded memories."

He took a small step closer, keeping her hand cradled in his. "You're not a stand-in, Lisa. You're a new light in my life, a happy surprise I never thought I'd find again." He saw a tear trace down Lisa's cheek as she softly expressed her need for something real, not just grand gestures. David felt a clench in his heart, realizing his romantic display might have overshadowed the sincerity he intended to convey. Lisa hesitated, her voice laced with cautious hope. "I feared I was just a salve for your past. Yet, hearing you now, there's a part of me daring to believe in more..." She exhaled a shaky breath. "I know what we have is real. I'm so sorry I ever doubted you."

David reached out, his fingers gently encircling her hand. "I might have overdone it," he admitted, his voice tinged with vulnerability. "But my feelings for you are as real as it gets."

The music faded to a soulful lament as David and Lisa stood hand in hand and gazed at each other. An understanding passed between them in the wordless moment, a promise to face fears and doubts together from now on. No more running from misunderstandings.

Then Lisa stepped into David's arms, melting against him like she belonged there. The dam inside him broke. He clung to her slender frame, awash with relief that he hadn't lost her. Her floral scent mingled with the night blooms surrounding them.

"I've missed you," he murmured against her hair. She tilted her face up to meet his gaze. The sheen of tears still glistened on her cheeks, but her smile was radiant. "No more running away?" he whispered.

"Never again," Lisa vowed.

David hesitated, his hands hovering near her face. The night air was charged with an electric current of unspoken words and pent-up emotions. Gently, he brushed his thumbs across her cheeks, tracing the path of her tears. His touch was a question, and her slight nod, an answer. The moment lingered, suspended in time, as they stood on the precipice of a new beginning. As their lips met, it was more than a mere kiss; it was a profound declaration, a melding of past pain and future dreams. Each gentle press spoke of forgiveness, of lost time reclaimed, and uncharted paths to be journeyed together. The kiss deepened, a dance of shared soul-searching, an unspoken vow that they were no longer fragments of their past but architects of a shared future. Lisa's response was a soft surrender, a yielding not just to his embrace but to the vulnerability and hope that shimmered between them. Gently, she leaned into him, her entire being unfolding in trust, her once-guarded heart now open and vulnerable in his presence. When their lips finally parted, it was as if they emerged from a cocoon of their own making. A soft gasp escaped Lisa as she rested her head against David's chest, her arms encircling him in a tender embrace. In the silence that followed, their shared breaths were whispers of a newfound commitment.

"This is where I belong," she said softly.

David kissed the top of her hair. "No doubts?"

She lifted her face to his again, love shining in her eyes. "None," she whispered.

The candles perfumed the night air with the scent of new possibilities. Holding Lisa close, David knew his life could never be the same. The past would linger, but the future gleamed bright with hope.

Together, they turned and walked hand in hand into the candle-lit garden and the promise of a new life built between two once solitary souls.

Epilogue: Jack

The air at the Constantia Corner Café was alive with the rich, velvety notes of jazz, each chord weaving through the warm, dimly lit space, caressing the vintage bookshelves and dancing over the well-worn wooden floors. Jack leaned against the polished wood counter, the deep, earthy scent of freshly brewed coffee mingling with the faint trace of lemon polish used on the aged wood, a comforting and familiar blend that spoke of many years and many stories. As owner of the café for over two decades, he had memorized every corner, from the vintage bookshelves to the framed photos of jazz legends adorning the walls. Tonight, his gaze settled on one particular table near the modest stage.

Lisa Marshall and David Pace sat closely together, heads bent in intimate conversation. Jack smiled, warmth spreading through his chest. He had orchestrated their first meeting here months ago, subtly ensuring they shared a table during the café's popular Jazz Night. From that spark, a relationship had bloomed, kindled by café get-togethers and Jack's gentle encouragements.

Observing them now, Jack couldn't help but think, *Who knew my café was better at matchmaking than most dating apps?* He chuckled to himself, marveling at how two wounded souls had found refuge in each other right here. He had recognized in Lisa and David a similar aura of cautious optimism. Their shared love of jazz had provided common ground to nurture a deeper connection.

As Jack lost himself in thought, a familiar voice called out, "Hey, Jack! Any chance for a top-up on this magic brew?"

Chuckling, Jack turned to see Mr. Hernandez, a regular, holding up his empty cup with a dramatic flourish. "Coming right up, but only if you promise to keep those dad jokes in check," Jack replied, his eyes twinkling with mirth.

Mr. Hernandez feigned a wounded look, placing a hand over his heart. "Jack, I'm hurt! My jokes are a classic—just like your jazz," he quipped with a laugh.

Then, shifting his tone to one of genuine appreciation, he added, "Speaking of which, another excellent jazz performance tonight. You always bring in marvelous talent."

"Happy to hear it!" Jack replied jovially. "I've got my eye on a few new musicians I think folks will enjoy."

Their chat ventured from jazz to rugby, with Mr. Hernandez passionately defending his favorite team. "Alright, I'll leave you to your heated debate with yourself," Jack joked, patting him on the back before weaving through the tables, exchanging quick, friendly banter with the staff.

Strolling through the café, Jack greeted everyone with his usual flair. "No, we haven't started charging for smiles yet," he quipped to a group of newcomers, who laughed as they settled more comfortably into their chairs. Near the piano, Jack paused, catching Dianne's eye. "That new batch of cinnamon rolls is outdoing itself," he called across the room.

She smiled back, "It's the jazz that's inspiring me, Jack!" He still marveled at the journey that had led him here. Twenty years ago, his military career had ended abruptly due to an injury. Adrift and uncertain, he had stumbled upon this charming but run-down building. With some vision and a sizeable loan, he transformed it into a cozy community hub.

Now, he felt fortunate to be even a small part of so many people's stories.

As he watched patrons lost in quiet conversations, Jack acknowledged a familiar affection stirring within for the café's talented pastry chef. Her chestnut waves perfectly framed kind green eyes. More than once, he had considered pursuing a deeper bond beyond their professional friendship. But a nagging hesitation held him back. Jack caught her eye once again from across the room, their gaze holding for a moment longer than usual. He sighed, a mix of longing and hesitation, before shaking his head with a small smile. "Not today," he murmured to himself, but the glimmer in his eye suggested a different tomorrow.

The robust aroma of deeply roasted coffee beans swept through the café, momentarily overpowering the enticing whispers of vanilla and cinnamon that usually floated in from Dianne's bustling bakery corner. It mingled with the earthy notes drifting in from the small garden. Jack breathed it all in, appreciating how every element blended to create the café's singular charm. Even the grooves etched into the wood floors whispered tales of the countless customers who had passed through.

A sudden burst of laughter erupted from a table near the open patio doors, where the cool evening breeze slipped in, bringing with it a hint of the night-blooming jasmine from the garden outside, mingling seamlessly with the café's vibrant atmosphere. He recognized two of the café's regulars. Rebecca's eye for antiques would perfectly complement Steve's love of history. Watching Steve and Rebecca, Jack mused, *If I had a dollar for every match I've made here...* His eyes twinkled at the thought as he mentally started planning the next 'accidental' encounter.

The saxophone's crisp notes cut through the ambient noise, each soulful melody rising and falling like a heartfelt confession, recapturing Jack's attention and drawing him back into the timeless rhythm of the jazz that was the café's heartbeat. On stage, the musician swayed as he coaxed soulful melodies from the brass instrument. Jack allowed the music to transport him back through decades of Jazz Nights. Over the years, the performances had ranged from mellow and nostalgic to bold and innovative. Yet jazz remained the unchanging heartbeat of his humble establishment.

As the last call approached, the music tapered into softer, melancholy tunes. The comforting aroma of coffee dissipated as patrons finished their final sips. Yet the warmth of community and connection lingered. This sanctuary Jack had built sheltered so many pivotal moments, from first meetings kindled over coffee to proposals and celebrations of every kind.

Glancing back at Lisa and David, Jack couldn't resist wandering over. "You two are becoming quite the fixture here," he observed, a warm smile on his face.

"Must be something in your coffee, Jack," Lisa replied with a playful wink, her eyes glinting with mirth. "It's absolutely irresistible." He felt that familiar swell of pride in seeing how his subtle matchmaking had helped unite two kindred spirits. Their ease and obvious affection were a testament to the power of empathy, forgiveness, and new beginnings. Not for the first time, Jack contemplated his unconventional role. What began on a whim had evolved into heartfelt efforts to connect patrons who seemed compatible. Nurturing real relationships took insight, patience, and care. He aimed to ignite sparks between people, but the rest was up to them. Fortunately, Lisa and David had embraced the potential and put in the hard work.

As Jack started tidying up, he chatted with the remaining customers. "Hope you enjoyed the music tonight," he said to a young couple.

"We loved it, Jack. This place is something special," they responded, their smiles genuine and appreciative.

He stacked chairs, wiped down tables, and ensured the garbage was taken out back. Soon the bustling café would grow quiet and dark, awaiting the new stories that tomorrow would bring. After cashing out the register, Jack glanced around once more at the empty space, taking in every detail that made this place so special to the community. He still remembered the scent of fresh paint when he had renovated years ago. Now, the tables showed spots of wear and each decor item whispered its own tale. The patina of age and use added to the café's charm.

With a satisfied nod, Jack switched off the remaining lights and stepped outside. A light evening breeze ruffled his hair as he locked the door. For a moment he simply stood, hands in pockets, gazing at the darkened windows. A contented feeling blossomed in his chest. The café had become far more than just a business venture. Within its walls, people found connection, solace, inspiration, and love. And he took pride in cultivating that.

As he strolled to his car, the faint scent of coffee and spices still clung to his shirt. The notes of jazz seemed to linger in the air around him. Tomorrow would bring new customers and new stories waiting to unfold. But tonight, Jack's thoughts glowed with quiet celebration of this humble community hub he had built.

MOCHA MOMENTS

He knew Lisa and David's love story was just one of many poignant tales that had blossomed within the café's walls. And there would be many more to come. Tomorrow, he would unlock the doors again, welcoming all seeking fellowship over coffee, among worn wooden tables under the gentle café lights.

For now, he would head home, his soul nourished from an evening at the heart of this place he so loved.

Leave a Review

Reviews are appreciated and welcome. :)

A review can be any length, from long to short or in between. Even a star rating is wonderful.

Thank you!

Get Your Free Book!

Sign up for my newsletter and as a thank-you, I'll send you a free novella.

It's a story close to my heart, filled with the kind of genuine, later-in-life romance that I love writing about.

Plus, you'll get a regular dose of updates, insights, and maybe a few surprises along the way.

No spam, just stories.

Interested?

Sign up and let's dive into this journey together.

Read More By Nina

Constantia Corner Café Series

Cappuccino Kisses

Mocha Moments

Burger Wine Estate Series

The Vintage of Love

The Stormy Path to Love

The Secret of Love

The Sweet Treat of Love

MOCHA MOMENTS

The Patience of Love

Burger Wine Estate Series Boxset: Books 1 to 5

The Magic Matchmaker Agency Series

Joseph

James

Joshua

Jake

John

Jason

The Magic Matchmaker Agency Boxset: 6 Stand-Alone Sweet Romance Novellas

About Nina Potter

Hi, I'm Nina Potter, a 59-years-young author of later-in-life romance novellas. My stories celebrate love, resilience, and personal growth, no matter your age.

Living in a small town in Southern Austria, I find inspiration in my own experiences and the enchanting world around me.

MOCHA MOMENTS

Before I started writing, I spent years working in the hotel and river cruise industries. This allowed me to explore the world and connect with people from all walks of life. These adventures have not only enriched my storytelling but also deepened my understanding of love, family, and self-discovery.

In my books, I strive to create authentic and relatable characters that resonate with readers. My stories are filled with emotional depth, genuine portrayals of mature relationships, and the transformative power of love, regardless of age or circumstance.

When I'm not writing my next novel, you can find me with my nose in a book, playing with my dog Theo, cooking for friends and family, or planning my next adventure to satisfy my wanderlust. I'm an active member of my community, participating in local book clubs and supporting cultural events that bring people together.

I invite you to join me on a journey of love, laughter, and self-discovery, as we explore the challenges and joys of finding romance in our later years through the eyes of my unforgettable characters.

Find me on Facebook, Instagram, TikTok, BookBub, Goodreads, Amazon, Substack.

If you liked this book, please take a few minutes to leave a review for it! Authors (me included!) really appreciate this, and it helps draw more readers to books they might like. Thanks!

Mocha Moments

Constantia Corner Café Book 2

Copyright © 2024 by Nina Potter

All rights reserved.

This book is a work of fiction. Names, characters, places, and incidents either are products of the author's imagination or are used fictitiously. Any resemblance to actual events, locales, or persons, living or dead, is entirely coincidental. No part of this book can be reproduced in any form or by electronic or mechanical means including information storage and retrieval systems, without the express written permission of the author. The only exception is a reviewer who may quote short excerpts in a review. Please purchase only authorized electronic editions, and do not participate in, or encourage, the electronic piracy of copyrighted materials. Your support of the author's rights is appreciated.

Cover-Photo: www.depositphotos.com

Cover designed by GetCovers

Formatted with Atticus

Edited by Kimberly Dawn

First Edition January 2024

Made in the USA
Columbia, SC
07 January 2024